For Florence and all the neighbors, who are like family.
—A.P.

For Devera and to all of the people in our neighborhood that make it home.
And to Nidhi and Leela, many thanks for the inspiration.
—S.K.

THIS IS A BORZOI BOOK PUBLISHED BY ALFRED A. KNOPF

Text copyright © 2022 by Alexandra Penfold
Jacket art and interior illustrations copyright © 2022 by Suzanne Kaufman

Visit us on the Web! rhcbooks.com

Educators and librarians, for a variety of teaching tools, visit us at RHTeachersLibrarians.com

Library of Congress Cataloging-in-Publication Data
Names: Penfold, Alexandra, author. | Kaufman, Suzanne, illustrator.
Title: All are neighbors / Alexandra Penfold ; [illustrated by] Suzanne Kaufman.
Description: First edition. | New York: Alfred A. Knopf, [2022]
Audience: Ages 4–8. | Audience: Grades K–1. | Summary: "When a new family moves in, the whole
neighborhood comes together to celebrate what makes their community diverse and special."
—Provided by publisher.
Identifiers: LCCN 2021056831 (print) | LCCN 2021056832 (ebook) | ISBN 978-0-593-42998-3
(hardcover) | ISBN 978-0-593-42999-0 (library binding) | ISBN 978-0-593-43000-2 (ebook)
Subjects: CYAC: Stories in rhyme. | Communities—Fiction. | Neighbors—Fiction. |
LCGFT: Stories in rhyme. | Picture books.
Classification: LCC PZ8.3.P376 Ali 2022 (print) | LCC PZ8.3.P376 (ebook) | DDC [E]—dc23

The text of this book is set in 16/22-point Corporative Soft.
The illustrations were created using acrylic paint, ink, crayon,
and collage with Adobe Photoshop.
Book design by Martha Rago

MANUFACTURED IN CHINA
10 9 8 7 6 5 4 3 2 1
First Edition

Alexandra Penfold Suzanne Kaufman

All Are Neighbors

Alfred A. Knopf   New York

What is a community?

It's a place for you and me.

Come along and you'll see.
We all are neighbors here.

We start our days in different ways.
Some go to work and others stay.

We're here for each other, come what may.
We all are neighbors here.

Let's go walking down our street.
Friends and neighbors here to greet.

Oh so many folks to meet.
We all are neighbors here.

What is a community?
It's a place for you and me.

Come along and you'll see.
We all are neighbors here.

A friendly smile, a familiar face.
Helping hands, just in case.

Taking care of our shared space.

We all are neighbors here.

We can help each other along.
Building bonds that are strong.

So everyone knows that they belong.
We all are neighbors here.

What is a community?
It's a place for you and me.

Come along and you'll see.
We all are neighbors here.

The sound of music in the street.
The scent of goodies ready to eat.

Feeling at home and complete.
We all are neighbors here.

This is our community.

We celebrate diversity.

all are neighbors here.

There's a place for *everybody.*